The Movie of Life
and other Short Stories

Discover Other Titles by Nate Henderson

Ideas on the Essentials

The Hopeful Bowl

Coming Soon:

Living in the Age of Information

Ideas on Life

The Outsider

The Wisdom of Life

The Movie of Life

and other Short Stories

Nate Henderson

Edited by Ashlynn Stewart

Jihona Publishing

Published by Jihona at Smashwords

www.jihona.net

Copyright 2015 Nate Henderson

ISBN (print): 978-0-9925204-3-4

Cover by SelfPubBookCovers.com/XanderWiersma

CONTENTS

INTRODUCTION BY THE AUTHOR

Short stories are a writer's project, providing an author. the space to put the many ideas circulating inside his head onto the page. Like any story, they start with the seed of an idea which is then extrapolated, and eventually presented to you, the reader. A short story contains characters and plots that are as dear to the author as those in a full length novel. They are still meticulously written, re-written and edited until they form a final product, ready to be shared with the world.

This selection of short stories was written while working on numerous other projects, both fiction and non-fiction. It was not a pre-meditated process, and for that reason the stories are not related, or even set in the same world or time that we live in. Yet all these stories were born from the same idea; that any individual has the capacity to change the world. The characters in these stories leave their mark on the world they live in, and they leave their mark on the people they meet on their journey. For some, these journeys are long and for others they are short. Some leave lasting impressions on the entire world, and others on just one person.

The first four stories in this collection are traditional short stories, while the final is a slightly longer novella. These stories have no greater meaning that the joy of storytelling. So please enjoy them, relate to them, and be inspired by them.

Nate.

A MAN NAMED ALEX

George was looking at his order sheets. He needed more coffee beans, and more flour. His customers had really been enjoying his homemade buttercream cake. George had to admit that it was pretty good. His home, the small settlement of Darington, was located some hours away from the closest major city, and most of his customers were farmers from the surrounding district.

George was in his mid-thirties. He had arrived in this town about three years ago, right after the collapse of the revolution against the national government, a repressive regime that had swept into power like an invading force and crushed all major resistance. This town, being so far away from the main centres of power, had not been very involved in the war. With his classic good looks and cavalier attitude, people had assumed George would cause trouble when he first arrived in the town. But instead George had bought a shop which had remained empty during the war. He slept upstairs in a small studio apartment and had opened up a café downstairs. While he was involved with the community and was one of them, he also kept mainly to himself.

Despite this, after three years the people had adopted George as one of their own.

"George dear, when are you going to choose one of our lovely young lasses and settle down with her?" Betty was a kindly old lady, complete with a walking stick and oversized glasses. She had immigrated from overseas and had come to this town over 40 years ago. She was about as local as you could get, having married a local man and gone on to raise three children, one of whom was the mayor of Darington.

Chuckling, George replied, "One day Betty. I am just trying to get this business running smoothly and then I will choose someone."

"Life will fly by you dear if you aren't careful. You are not a young man anymore George. And you need a wife."

"The usual today Betty?" George replied, trying in earnest to change the topic.

"Yes dear, just some of your lovely buttercream cake and a tea." George went behind the counter to prepare Betty's daily morning tea. He always gave her a discount, but Betty always left some extra cash on the table as she left. George really did love life in Darington. No one ever asked why he came there, or what he had done in his past, but the people had accepted him, and he them.

George was so engrossed by his own thoughts, that it was only when he was bringing over the cake and tea for Betty did he notice that she was focusing intently on something outside. "That man outside will be bad news George. Be careful, it looks like he is heading this way." Looking up, George noticed a young man in a leather jacket with a hard face getting out of a nice looking car parked outside the café. He was clearly from the city. The people of Darington were always wary of city folk, and this man looked like someone with a purpose. The man entered the store, nodded towards Betty and George and took a seat at the back of the café. George walked over to the man. "Good day sir, what can I get you?"

The man replied, "A coffee, and some of that nice looking cake over there please."

George went back behind the counter to prepare the man's coffee and cake. Glancing up, he noticed the man was staring fixedly at him. Finishing up and walking over, George gave the man his coffee and cake. "Here you go sir. Enjoy."

The man took a bite from the cake. "This is fantastic cake," he exclaimed, a little louder than necessary.

Betty, who had been pretending to read her magazine, glared at the man before returning to her magazine, one ear turned to hear what the man might say next.

"What brings you all the way to Darington? This place is not usually on anyone's way to anywhere, particularly not for city folk," George said. In retrospect he realised this question was possibly a little abrupt, but there was something about this man that didn't add up.

The man, still intent on the cake, said in between bites, "You know, I have tasted cake exactly like this before. It was famous during the war. There was this leader who gave a very similar recipe to the troops, and everyone would bake and eat it. You see, it has very few ingredients, and can be easily transported."

The man stopped eating his cake, and looking directly at George said, "Famously, this leader was not seen again after the failure of the revolution. Many people said it was because the man was killed by the authorities. But there are those that think he escaped and made a new life for himself."

Backing away, George replied, "The war is over, and the revolutionaries lost. But I am glad my cake could give you some good memories. Enjoy."

George turned from the man back towards the counter.

4

He was rattled by the man's comments but tried to conceal his feelings. After ten minutes counting stock (in fact he had counted the same stock three times), George felt brave enough to steal a glance in the direction of the man, and was relieved to see that he was reading a book while sipping his coffee.

Half an hour later Betty said her farewell, and slowly made her way to the door. As George was holding the door for Betty, she looked up at him and said, "Just remember dear, you are one of us, and whatever that past life of yours was, it is just that. In the past." With this, Betty turned and left. Fortunately five minutes later the man got up from his seat, tipped his head at George, and left the store. But instead of heading to his car he turned and walked up the street. George tried to push the man to the back of his mind, but his words kept repeating in his head, daring him to close the store and do something rash. Luckily, George had little time to be distracted by such thoughts, as the lunchtime rush was starting. He really needed to hire an assistant.

By the time the man re-entered the café just an hour before George was due to close up, George had forgotten the morning's events. The man was much more polite this time, coming up to the counter where George was busy making coffee for a family of four.

"Your cake was so good this morning that I thought I would come back for more before the trip back to the city," the man said.

"Sure, would you also like another coffee?" George asked warily.

"Yes that would be great, I'll take a seat over there." Leaving the counter the man took his seat and began reading his book.

An hour later the man was the only customer left in the café. "We will be closing soon sir," George told him. The man replied, "I was hoping to chat with you about something. Would you mind if I waited until you close, and then we can talk?"

George's senses were on alert and he wanted nothing more than to show the man out, but he also knew that the man was unlikely to leave town until he had spoken his piece, so he simply nodded and went about finishing his daily duties. About half an hour later, George walked over to the man and sat down.

"What would you like to talk about?" George asked, a little more bluntly than he'd intended. The man paused before answering, "I like this town; it's very peaceful. I can understand why you moved here."

He continued, "I apologise for not introducing myself before. My name is Sam and I am from the city as I'm sure you guessed. I was part of the revolutionary army, before its great defeat three years ago. While many were quickly absorbed back into society, there was a small band of us who have continued the fight. And we have made inroads, we have reformed and regrouped." Sam was now looking directly at George.

"Why are you telling me this? I know the history, but what you are saying is treason," George said.

"Treason maybe, but it's necessary and that's the truth. You know, I spent the day asking the people in this town about you. They were naturally suspicious of me and didn't give me much information but I did find out a few things. They love you here and consider you one of their own. They want you to run for the local council. They say that you are a natural leader, someone who inspires people. I remember that people always did see you as a natural born leader... Alex."

There was a flicker of recognition in George's eyes when Sam said the name Alex. Sam continued, "You were the leader of our revolution. Your name is in the history books. There is still a large reward for your capture. Of course, the people in this town would never give you up. They actually supported us during the war and provided us with food. But I guess you already knew that when you chose this town as your hideaway."

George knew he had a choice. Sam had discovered his true identity. As was his natural inclination when he was the leader of the revolution, he took a chance on this stranger and finally spoke about the things he'd been keeping to himself for more than three years.

"We lost the war and the revolution was crushed. While I can understand why you continue to fight against our corrupt government, I can't get involved in all that again. I have made a new life here, so let me live it. I like what I do, it matters to people, and it matters to me. I am sorry, but the past must remain the past"

Sam leaned forward. "Alex, you must return and lead us once again. You will bring hope to the people, a symbol of defiance that can't be destroyed, just like when you led us before. There was a reason you were our leader then, and those reasons haven't changed. We need you to help us overthrow this regime, and put the power in the hands of the people."

Sam looked out the window and said, "I have booked myself into the local inn for the night. I will come by in the morning and if you still don't want to join us, I will leave and you will never see me again. No one knows you are here, and there is no reason they ever have to." With that, Sam stood up and left the café.

George, who had been Alex in his previous life, spent the night considering his options. He was not blind to what was happening outside of his town. While he led a decent life in Darington, he knew that life for most, particularly in the large population centres, was hard. He had kept up with the news and had watched with dismay as people he knew had been publicly executed for their involvement in the revolution. Over the years, there had been occasions when his own name had been mentioned on the news, connected with terrible things the regime was trying to pin on him. But he loved his simple life. He'd been so young when he took command of the revolution, had made so many mistakes and done too many terrible things. He had led so many brave men and women to their deaths. If he left now, he would never be able to share this peaceful life with some young lass, as Betty had put it. He imagined how idyllic it would be to share this café with that someone and live a normal life. A rewarding life.

After a fairly sleepless night, George went through the routine of opening up the café, still undecided on a course of action. He was therefore surprised when Betty entered the café ten minutes after he opened.

"George dear, grab yourself a coffee and come have a chat," she told him

He did as she asked, saying, "What's wrong Betty?"

"Dear, that man that was here yesterday. I know who he is, and more importantly what he wants." She looked at him soberly.

"Betty, how could you know such things?" George asked.

"Because, George, when you came to this town three years ago, my oldest son recognised you. He was a young officer and had seen you once and knew your face. And whenever someone asked too many questions about you, or wondered why you suddenly arrived just as the revolution crumbled, my son helped to keep your identity a secret. We know what you did. We know the sacrifices you made. And I know the choice you have to make today, whether to stay or go."

George was shocked, amazed and more confused than ever. But Betty pressed on, "If there is something I have learned in my long life dear, it's this. We define our lives by the things we do, not the things we wish we had done.

There is a good life waiting for you here."

Without even touching her tea, Betty left the café.

George didn't know what to think. Should he become Alex and take up a fighting life again, or should he remain in Darington? George looked around at the life he had built. It was truly wonderful to have this life, to be a part of this community. But he also knew that it was not in his nature to sit idly by while there was injustice in the world, especially now that he knew there was something he could do about it. George made a decision, closed the store and went up to his studio apartment. When Sam came to the café an hour later, it was Alex, not George, who was waiting for him.

DREAMS AND REALITY

I am sick. They say that I'm dying. But that doesn't mean I can't still dream.

I dream of being a princess named Rose in a faraway land where rolling hills give way to lush meadows where horses graze. I live in a big wonderful castle, full of exquisite paintings, magical carpets and many servants. When I look out my window I see the village below, with its cobblestone roads, wooden cottages and the market, which is the busiest part of the town. Merchants are yelling out their wares to the unsuspecting customer. Every now and then, I see a young boy, picking the pocket of the rich. I envy this boy, with the freedom to do as he pleases. I am a princess but I am also a prisoner. Sometimes, he looks up at me and smiles devilishly. I do not know if he sees me or is simply looking up and praying to the gods. One day a solider rushes at him and knocks the boy to the ground. More soldiers come and they grab the boy and head towards the castle. I hurriedly make my way down to the great hall to find out what is happening. He is brought up to the throne, and finally I see this boy, a man really, up close. For the first time I stare straight into his eyes.

They are a magical sparkling blue, but as I look the shimmer dies and is replaced with a terrible sadness. Judgement is passed and he is taken to the cells below the castle. That night I secretly make my way down to the cells. I find him chained to a wall and he knows who I am, the proud princess who stares down at the world from the safety of her castle. He thinks I turned him in and is spiteful towards me. "What would you know about my life, princess? You are free to do as you please, never having to bother about food or clothes. It is not that easy for the rest of us you know, who starve and freeze while your castle takes and takes and takes." He turns from me. I begin to protest, but the look in his eyes is angry, no hint of a sparkle left. I turn and slowly walk back up the stairs, thinking about how this castle divides the powerful from the rest. It seems we are both prisoners now.

Soon I will leave this world. The doctor says I have maybe a week. I am chained to this hospital, a prisoner. The sparkle in my eyes might have left, but at least I am still free to dream.

I dream of being in ancient China as the legendary fighter named Mei, the first female general of the imperial army. My reputation precedes me as an extraordinary fighter, and my army is sent throughout the land to defend the Emperor's rule and honour. I come from a noble family and was raised within the palace. From an early age I was fascinated with weapons and fighting. My family's prominent position at court and within the army meant that I could be trained as a soldier, as I wished. When I turned eighteen I passed the Jian Trials, the youngest to ever succeed, and was eventually promoted to general. I'm constantly reminded that I'm a woman intruding into the world of men, unlike the dainty subservient specimens in the Emperor's harem. Many have challenged me over the years seeking to prove that I am unworthy of my high position, certain that I tricked my way into power. I win most of these challenges but sometimes I let an opponent win in order to preserve his honour and to keep the peace. The Emperor is aware of this, and he has told me that he respects my selflessness. Rumours have been growing for some time about the Shui-He League, a rebel group intent on overthrowing the Emperor. The League is behind many violent incidents around the empire and they are growing in number. Their leader is a man named Feng, who is by all accounts a great fighter and a hero of the common people. For many years Feng has protested against the perceived injustices committed by the Emperor against his own people. He talks to angry crowds about repressive taxes and poor crop yields, imprisoned peasants and harsh laws. I knew that before long the Emperor would be forced to send me to deal with this threat. One day I gained information about the League's hiding place and was ordered to kill Feng and leave his body strung up in the imperial square for all to see. Alone, I am able to slip into their hideout undetected. I find Feng's private quarters, alert for any sign of a trap. He is standing unarmed in the centre of the room, his back to me and his head hanging down. I am confident that I can easily defeat him. Without turning around Feng speaks. "I knew the Emperor would send you to kill me. I will not fight back. I only request that you be quick." Curious, I ask, "Why will you not stop me?" He replies, "I will not raise a sword against my own blood." Angry at this cheap trick I come up behind him and force him to his knees, pressing my sword against his neck. Feng does not resist me and a splinter of doubt enters my mind. "Why do you call me blood? I have never even met you before today." He says, "It was predicted long ago that a twin brother and sister would be born who would destroy the unjust rule of the Emperor. When he learned of this prophecy, the

Emperor sent his assassins to kill all the twins in the land. Meanwhile the rebellion was growing stronger and our parents were heavily involved. They separated us and sent us to be raised by different families so that we would be kept safe. The League is strong now and with you by my side I know we could defeat the Emperor together." I could not believe what I was hearing. I walked around him to look at his face, and gasped. It was like looking into a mirror. Everything I thought I knew about myself was in doubt. I left Feng kneeling in his room and hurried back to the palace, determined to confront my family. They were very upset and decided that it was no longer safe for me at the palace. They smuggled me out and left me hidden with some friends at the edge of the city. That night the League launched an attack on the palace. Cries rang out in the night and the palace glowed orange from many fires. Worried about my family, I tried to sneak back into the palace to find them and get them to safety. As I passed the throne room, I caught a glimpse of the Emperor standing over a figure lying on the dais, an ornate dagger raised in his hand. There were many bodies lying all over the room. The Emperor shifted slightly and I saw that the figure was Feng. I cried out in horror and the Emperor turned to face me. In his distraction I saw Feng bring up his sword and run it through the Emperor, instantly killing him. I rushed over to the dais and saw that Feng was deeply wounded and very weak. I clung to him, not knowing what to do or what was going to happen. Feng died as dawn broke. That day was the beginning of a new era for our people. With the Emperor dead and the League in control of the palace, and with the backing of the general populace, the rebellion succeeded. As a leader in both worlds, general of the imperial army and sister of the League's commander, I was appointed Empress. I created new laws based on Feng's teachings and named the empire after him. The people were better off because of him, and although I felt I had not spent enough time with Feng, I never forgot him.

Mum cried when I told her this story but I told her that even after death you are still remembered, and even if you die young, you can still make a difference. I am not upset by the fact that my life will be short, because I have dreamed many different versions of my life, long and short. And I am still dreaming.

I dream of being a village girl named Kotix. My tribe is very isolated in the highlands of our remote country. My grandparents remember the old time when they did not know of anyone outside of the tribe. Then the white man came with his technology. My mother tells stories of a time of chaos when everything began changing. I was born into this new time, where tradition and progress warred. I dream of going to school and getting a job and becoming successful and famous. But I am not allowed to go to school. My brothers go off one by one, and I must stay home and learn the ways of the tribeswomen. Of course I still want to help out my family and help my mother with all the household chores, but I also want to learn new things. Every day, my brothers come home from school, and speak to one another in a new language that I can't understand. I am determined to learn about what my brothers are saying. So, every day I complete my chores really fast, and then I take out one of my brother's old school books and teach myself English. It is really hard and a slow process, but I never get tired of it. I begin to learn how to read, learning a word or two every day. After one year, I am able to read simple English texts. I hide the fact that I can read from my brothers, as they are not doing so well at school. I don't want them to get jealous of me and take away my books. One day I was reading and I was so absorbed in my study that I did not hear my mother come up behind me. She saw what I was doing and stopped in her tracks. She slowly backed away again, both surprised and proud at what she had witnessed. After that, I noticed that I was given less and less chores, but I didn't care since I had more time to dedicate to reading. My mother would occasionally sneak up behind me every now and then just to make sure that I was still reading. My mother began to leave my brothers' other school books around the house for me to find, and I was able to spend much of my time learning new things. After five years, I had managed to learn as much as my oldest brother, who had just completed primary school. My mother knew that my father and brothers would not be happy that a girl had learned so much, especially without any schooling. So one day she packed a bag with all the food and money in the house. She was going to tell my father that an unknown tribe had robbed the house and taken me with them. My mother was not going to stand by and see all my learning go to waste. She surprised me at my favourite hiding place where I was reading my forbidden books. I was so shocked that she had found out after all this time that I threw the book down and babbled excuses until I saw that my mother crying. "What is wrong mama?" I asked. My mother explained how proud she was of me and, handing me the bag, told me to go and never come back. She had one request, "Kotix, I want you to use your life to help other girls". With that she walked back to the house to make it look like it had been robbed. Crying, I grabbed the bag and took one last look at my mother. I turned around and I never looked back. And I never saw my mother or my home again.

I believe that the world is full of many moments and many choices, and sometimes the paths we choose can change our lives forever. There are so many stories I still wish to tell. I do not know where my own story will finish, and as I tell my mother, a story is more than just its ending. I think of life like a beautiful painting, full of colourful confusion close up, but creating an exquisite pattern once you look at the whole picture, a pattern that you are always aware of but maybe you haven't taken the time to try and understand. Our colourful splashes of life end up blending with the splashes of colour all those other lives that we touch. I like to think of my colour as a broad yellow stripe which tells everyone that even a life as short as mine can have a bright and lasting effect. As I look down, I see my mother crying, and I follow the arms of the angel, ready for my next dream.

THE FIRST HOUR

What would you do if you realised the world was ending? How would you respond? And what if your loved ones weren't with you? I know what that's like because it happened to me.

Earlier today, the sun was a vibrant orange colour, with little bits of red around the edges as it set behind the hills. The day had been a little humid, with some light rain, and the clouds stretched across the horizon like sheets in an unmade bed. Spread across the large plain that separated my mountain and the mountain opposite was the town closest to my secluded house. As I looked out at the beauty that was my daily view, a shiver ran down my spine and I had a strong feeling that this was the last sunset that I was ever going to see. I was right.

As twilight set in I went into the kitchen and started dinner. I was making ravioli, which is a favourite of mine, and especially of my fiancée Abigail, who was on a business trip. I loved my little kitchen, with its teak wooden benches, wooden floorboards, and a small stove powered by a small gas bottle that sat hidden under one of the benches. The rest of our home was similar in style, a small simple cabin made of wood, nestled into the side of the mountain. It already feels like a lifetime since I left my home, instead of just a few hours. The water for the ravioli began to boil, so I went over to take the lid off. That was when the rumbling began. At first it was faint like an airplane passing high overhead, but the rumbling quickly grew to a roar and then the whole house began to shake. I reached over just in time to turn off the stove before the water pot crashed to the floor, and I was forced to jump back. Items were falling off shelves and breaking, and then the power went out. I was stumbling around in the dark, hoping that the ceiling wouldn't fall in on me. Just when I was sure that the house would collapse the shaking finally stopped.

In the ensuing silence I realised that the whole day had been unusually quiet, without even birdsong to break up the monotony. I strained my ears for a sound, but heard nothing. None of the night insects or marsupials answered my silent prayer. I wished that even an annoying mosquito would come and bite me, just so that I would know that nothing had changed and that things were still normal. But there was only the oppressive silence.

I picked myself up off the floor and stumbled outside, expecting to see a huge hole in the world. But the sight that greeted me was far more spectacular. The sky had come to life and while the sun hadn't returned, the sky was all shades of red, orange and purple, all shifting and bleeding together. It was as if the sky was alive, but had been mortally wounded. I didn't understand what was going on. I looked down towards the town only to see most of the buildings were either destroyed or on fire. It did not even resemble a town, but rather a desolate wasteland. It looked like the end of the world. I turned to Abigail, but then I remembered that she was millions of miles away and with a sick feeling in my gut I realised that I was truly alone.

Abigail and I met five years ago. Our relationship had grown stronger with time, and I hate it when we're not together. If you have ever loved someone, you will know that when you're feeling sad or scared, or when you're sick or tired, that's when you especially need your other half to support you, and to reassure you that everything is going to be okay. I needed Abigail to tell me in her very practical way that everything was okay and there was no reason to panic.

At the thought of Abigail, I picked up my phone and tried to call her, but the call wouldn't connect. I had no way of knowing what had happened or whether she was alright. What if a similar earthquake had struck her hotel and it had collapsed? What if her city was in chaos, people running everywhere, phones not working and half the buildings on fire? What if she needed me? I wasn't thinking too clearly at that moment but I knew one thing – I had to get to her. I told myself that I could easily find her since I needed desperately to believe that I'd see her again.

With a newfound determination I strode back into the house and grabbed a backpack lying on the floor. While the electricity had not come back on, the shifting lights in the sky were bright enough to see by. Into the backpack I threw supplies of dry biscuits and water, some toiletries, a spare change of clothes, a torch and some money –anything that was lying around and looked useful. Looking at the table next to my bed I instinctively grabbed my multipurpose portable charger and shoved it into my pocket. Luckily I had charged it that day. Little did I realise the value of power in a world turned upside down.

I ran out to my car, a four-wheel drive designed for the tough roads where I lived. The keys, as always, were in the sunshade. Looking back now it seems strange that I rushed off into the dark with little preparation while the world was ending around me. I had no idea where to go or how I was going to get to Abigail, but my fast action saved my life. I didn't hear the fire at first but a hurricane of red flames was racing down the mountainside, engulfing everything in its path. Luckily it hadn't yet blocked the road but I needed to get out of there immediately. Throwing my gear into the backseat I started the car and took off, leaving a stream of dust in my wake. I don't know if the fire actually reached my house or miraculously passed by it. I guess I might never know, but I like to think the house was spared, and will be waiting when I return with Abigail.

I turned on the radio and the presenter confirmed my worst suspicions, that the earthquake which had destroyed my whole town in just a few moments was in fact part of a shockwave that had reverberated around the entire world. Whole cities had been levelled or flooded in the resulting tsunamis. Millions were dead. No one yet knew the cause or the extent of the damage. Abigail's city wasn't mentioned. It didn't occur to me at the time, but I don't know why the radio stations were still broadcasting, or how the presenter knew precisely where and how the earthquake had hit. But he kept me company for the drive into town.

I arrived at the edge of town and slowed down, switching the radio off. The scene that greeted my eyes was horrendous. There were dozens of people lying dead in the street, covered in blood and illuminated only by the eerily shifting glow from the sky. While it was obvious some people had been shot, it was also clear that others had died from different causes. Some had limbs missing and others had lacerations all over their bodies. I kept thinking that none of it could possibly be real because it was too hard to explain. To this day I am still not sure what happened there, and I can tell you I was not about to leave the safety of the car to find out. But it seemed that not everyone had died. Ahead of me on the road was a large group of people who had noticed my car and were pointing at me. They didn't look friendly. I felt very uneasy and I decided I had seen enough. I sped down a side road, took a few more turns, and then drove onto the expressway that led to the next city. I didn't know what would greet me there but it seemed better than hanging around the town.

Speeding recklessly down the expressway I thought about what I had witnessed in the town. It was unnatural. Dead people on the street and no sign of the police or army. It was clear the earthquake and fire around my house had not been normal, and something else must have happened in the town, something else that had caused the gruesome deaths of all those people. What if that something had already visited the city, what would I find there?

I didn't have long to find out. I made it to the city in record time without encountering any other vehicles. When I arrived the city appeared to be empty though moderately intact. As I drove through the streets I saw vandalised shops, downed trees and burning cars. There were a few people sprawled on the pavements, limbs missing, their blood seeping into the sewer drains, some with burns all over their bodies and others with makeshift weapons protruding unnaturally. There were not nearly enough bodies to account for the vast population here, so where was everybody else? Could all this really have happened in less than a couple of hours? It was clear that whatever had happened was far more than just a normal earthquake. And while there were some small fires, there was also no evidence of the giant wave of fire that I had seen engulf my mountain. It was all so strange and I wondered suddenly why the radio presenter had made no mention of any bizarre deaths or unexplainable events.

Suddenly I spotted a small group of men crossing the road up ahead and I slowed down instinctively and turned my headlights off. I desperately hoped they wouldn't see me as they had a violent look about them. The group were obviously being led by one man in front who held a shotgun. The others all carried different weapons, mostly crowbars, steel rods and other improvised weapons. Perhaps this was the group that had brutally killed the people I had seen on the side of the street? The group did see me however and they began rushing towards my car. I threw the car in reverse and sped away down another street. There was another gang ahead so I took the next side road, not wanting to be caught between two violent gangs. I saw a sign pointing towards the harbour and took that road, thinking there might be a chance of getting on a boat so I could start my search for Abigail. After all, my car wouldn't be able to run on half a tank forever, and it didn't seem safe enough to stop anywhere for gas. Besides it would be faster to sail across the strait than drive around it.

Aside from the two groups of men I had just encountered and the dead on the side of the road, I had not seen a soul since entering the city. Where had everyone gone? This city had housed millions of people and people don't just disappear into thin air. I felt I was leaving with so many more questions than answers. I parked the car right in front of the harbour, thinking that no one was going to give me a ticket for illegal parking today. I grabbed my bag, locked the doors and pocketed the keys, and briskly walked towards the ferry. I saw a uniformed man coming out of the ticket office, a large backpack on his back and two smaller bags in his hands. He was probably the ferry captain and he looked nervous. He was about to make a run for his ship when I approached him and asked if I could go with him across the strait. He told me to go away and kept looking around anxiously, but I kept talking about my fiancée and begging him to take pity on me and he eventually agreed to take me. I think he just wanted to get out of there as fast as possible.

He told me there were gangs of fanatical young men with weapons who were rounding people up and telling them not to leave the city, but to await God's final judgement. I heard shouts in the distance and saw fear in the captain's eyes. We made a run for the ship, but the group saw us and gave chase. We were on the pier when the leader shouted at us to stop or they would shoot. Terrified we turned around while the gang caught up to us and surrounded us. They asked us why we were leaving and the captain tried to reason with them, telling them we both had family we needed to visit, but it was clear that these guys were not interested in listening. I stepped forward to try and reason with the leader but someone must have thought I was threatening him because a second later pain exploded from the back of my head. I fell to my hands and knees and blood started to drip onto the ground. My portable charger had fallen out of my pocket and had landed at the feet of the leader. He picked it up gleefully. I realised that the power in the charger was probably as valuable as food or water at this point, since there didn't seem to be any power in the city anymore.

"You can have it!" I said. "And here, have the keys to my car, it has half a tank. Please, just let us go," I begged. The leader didn't say anything and then finally spoke, "Don't come back you hear? This is our city now. Come on boys, let's go." Then they left us and headed back towards the parking lot. We boarded the ferry and the captain immediately had us cast off and turned the ferry towards the mouth of the harbour.

And so now my diary is up to date. It has been a little over five hours since the earthquake, but it feels like a lifetime. I am sailing across the strait, towards Abigail. I know where she is, and I hope she is waiting for me. But if not, I will not stop searching until I find her. I can see dark storm clouds ahead so I had better go back up on deck and help the captain and crew. I will write more when I have a chance.

☐

THE ARCHIVIST

The archivist consulted his notes again briefly even though he would have known what was written there with his eyes closed. He gazed lovingly at the excavation site which reconnected him with his ancestry, as well as ensuring a healthy pay check from the government. The archivist was one of only a few in his profession. His job was to look into the background of this recently discovered historical site. "This discovery confirms my theories," he thought excitedly to himself. His work mainly covered the Millennial Period and he promulgated several theories about how humanity had gone to war over resources, which had essentially led to the downfall of their civilisation.

The excavated site the archivist was currently looking into was the largest one ever discovered – one of the fabled Metropolises that the Millennials had been forced to build to deal with overpopulation. The idea of the world not being large enough to contain humanity seemed laughable today. The site was made up of a number of extremely tall buildings located on a very small area of land. Rock formations in the area indicated that this land had once been surrounded entirely by water. Tests had revealed this site was only 600 years old, so that meant it was still used right up until the Crisis.

The archivist had been tasked with uncovering information about the past and adding to the archives in the capital city, about two days away by boat. The world had changed significantly since the Red Crisis. What had caused the Crisis was not clear but what he did know was that it had almost destroyed all human life and altered the world's land masses significantly. It was part of his job to unearth clues and try to explain what happened. Fascinated by the past, the archivist had taken on this role with great passion. It was only in the last fifty years that humans had begun the search for the ancient wonders of the past. The Oral Histories provided no real evidence to support the more popular myths about the Millennials, and many people were content to leave this tainted past behind. But an earthquake fifty years ago had ruptured a mountain and revealed a half-buried tower, intact and gleaming unnaturally in the sunlight. The discovery had sent everyone into a frenzy. Since then, many sites had been discovered and unearthed but none of the sites found on this continent had been as large as the one the archivist now looked at. His initial thought was that this island, along with its entire civilisation, had collapsed not long after the Crisis and any survivors had probably fled.

The excavation crew had left for the day. Large pieces of the stone equipment sat silently where their owners had last used them. They encircled the site, protecting it like silent guard dogs, a warning that this area was claimed. The gentle wind that blew around the towers added an eerie whistling sound so that the entire place felt like an alien world. The government had put a lot of money into this project, and the equipment used here was the best in the world. It took a lot of manpower and many hours of manually moving the different digging and hauling components of the machines, turning the winches and securing the different ropes. It may not be Millennial technology but it was still better than anywhere else in the world.

Some of the intact buildings that had been excavated soared towards the sky, but what was incredible was that they seemed to extend even further down into the earth, and what could be seen was merely the tip of the building itself. It was almost certain that their equipment would not be up to the task of clearing the site all the way to the bottom of the structures, but even this small glimpse was a clear indication of the wonders of the old world. It was not clear to the archivist exactly how the Millennials had built these towers. Dust from the atmosphere had since coated the towers in white and they now resembled the ghosts of a once-great civilisation.

The archivist had explored each of the five buildings that his team had so far uncovered, gaining access through square holes cut into their sides. These holes were too precise for the cutting to have been done by hand, and there were rows and rows of them. He had meticulously recorded his findings for the Archives, and had already made a preliminary assessment that many more of these buildings would be found in the surrounding hills. He surmised that each of these buildings had originally housed anywhere between five hundred to one thousand people, an unbelievable amount given his capital contained only one thousand people in total.

He had discovered what appeared to be communal

living areas which he supposed must have arisen from the lack of resources they were famous for. Whole families must have lived together, cramped into these small dwellings with only very thin walls to separate them from their neighbours. He found it hard to fathom the rationale for why the Millennials had lived so close to each other. The evidence pointing to the sheer amount of people who had lived on this island was remarkable, making it even more difficult to understand their society, and how it differed to his own. In the archivist's world, everyone had large divisions of land in their keeping and most chose to live separate lives, foraging and sustaining themselves as needed, unless they were raising a family. People did flock to the capital though because there were servants to cook for them as well as other convenient facilities. The archivist had a wonderful home on the edge of the meadow near the capital. It was peaceful there, and he realised suddenly that he missed his family.

If only all of the Millennial's records had not been lost in the Crisis, thought the archivist. It was inconceivable that there had not been archives or histories available, but they were yet to be found. Some people assumed there were other communication and recording techniques that were used back then, but those theories were considered fanciful. The archivist knew that paper was a precious commodity, and delicate, so it was easy to understand why it had all been destroyed. The capital's archives were considered extensive but even they only reached back 500 years or so. It was considered wasteful to make copies when there were so few trees, so it would set humanity back half a century if a natural disaster occurred which destroyed the ar52chives. Still, society functioned and those in power were hungry for any information about the past which could benefit them now. Especially when it came to technology. The archivist suspected the government was trying to recreate the technology so they could tap into the power of the Millennials.

The archivist had a good friend, a historian, who had recently written a book titled "The Era of Plenty" in which he discussed his own theories about the past, where advanced technology processes, systems and machines arose simultaneously with the abundance and availability of food, water and energy for all people. His theory of "Mass Production" was widely accepted as the most accurate picture of how this era must have operated and went some way towards populating the myths about the Millennials. In fact Mass Production had been one of the platforms of the new government's and was now something that the world's best minds were working on. It was generally believed that if society could replicate enough wonders from the Millennials world, then life would be infinitely better. But what if repeating past successes also meant repeating past mistakes? He felt that people dismissed the mystery and danger of the Crisis too easily these days.

Society was currently ruled by people who took a very singular view on the world: that they were at the start of another golden age of humanity. Golden ages of humanity had existed throughout history and the Millennials had simply been the most recent one. The (very few) books that had been found referred to earlier civilisations, but one could only guess when and where those had occurred. He didn't actually know what "golden" meant, so how could it be measured? How did they gain more technology, more food, water and shelter, and why were they always grabbing for more, more, more? And where had all this greed gotten them? When he was young, he had listened to the myths and stories of old civilisations passed down through the Oral Histories, and he had been fascinated by them ever since. His professional life had been based around providing information on how the Millennials worked in order to copy their greatness, but the more he researched, the more he started to question his missions. It was safer not to raise these concerns, so they archivist kept his questions to himself.

Lost in his reverie, the archivist had been walking aimlessly around site while the sun began to set. He realised he had entered a part of the Metropolis that was only partially uncovered. A landslide in this part of the site had accidently unearthed what would become the archivist's defining find, and would make him famous. He stood in front of an ornate building, wider and taller than any of the others. He walked between two grand birds covered with white dust, wings spread as if to welcome him into the building. He noticed an opening and unable to stop his heart from beating faster, stepped into the dark interior. The building was as grand inside as it was outside, with a high ceiling and an array of colourful pictures that were slowly peeling off the walls. The last rays of sunlight striped through the square holes in the building, lighting his way. The weight of the walls pressed down on him and he wondered how many levels below the ground the building went. The eerie silence made his spine tingle in fear. The archivist walked through room after room until he came to his first locked door. He grasped the handle and it snapped in his hand. He pushed at the door with all his strength, even though he wasn't sure why he needed to go in there. As it slowly opened, he felt musty air rushing past him, as if the room had been sealed. A glow from a central dome near the ceiling brightened until the room was bathed in artificial light and the archivist looked upon a room that held more books than he could have ever imagined. Scarcely able to contain his excitement at the secrets that could soon be revealed to him, he walked into the middle of the room. There was one table set up in the room, with a single book on it. Very carefully, the archivist opened the book. It was dated and appeared to be a journal, though the writing was neater and more precise than could ever be written by hand. Reading the first few pages, the archivist's eyes widened and he stared in disbelief as he finally found out what had caused the Red Crisis.

Humanity always looks for better and more plentiful sources of energy. In his own world, this was a preoccupation, with local furnaces the major source of energy for society, although there were plenty of people looking into better and more powerful energy sources. The journal spoke of the Millennials' obsession with creating infinite and more powerful sources of energy. Just below the earth's crust was an immense source of heat that could be turned into sustainable energy for millions. The Millennials drilled deep into the bedrock of the oceans, and tapped into that energy until every nation on earth was using it to power Metropolises, food generators and even advanced weaponry. Almost inevitably, there was a drilling disaster which rapidly caused global tectonic disruptions, which in turn created giant tsunamis and volcanic eruptions on every continent. These waves of water and lava swept away entire civilisations and destroyed entire sections of landmasses. It had been the end of humanity.

The archivist reverently held the journal in his hands. Here were the answers he had searched for his whole life. He took the book with him when he left the building. It was now almost completely dark, and the archivist needed to get back to the camp. It was not wise to be wandering around alone at night in this isolated place. The building, the sealed room, the books that the archivist had just found would fundamentally change his society forever, but would it be for the better? Would the government seek to cover up this information, or use it to make decisions that would chart a different course? Would they find a different way to create a golden age in society? He wasn't sure of the answers to these questions, but after all, his fascination was with the past. Let others worry about the future.

THE MOVIE OF LIFE

The movie of life, what a title. But it is an accurate title. For life, like a movie, has all the surprises of an opening, a middle and an end. Life is made up of an infinite amount of experiences, opportunities and surprises. But where to begin such an epic? By setting the scene.

The scene we are setting has the most beautiful and wondrous objects. There are the high peaks of mountains, crowned with snow and rock. The wide blue sky and ocean, reflecting each another, full of life, colour and ambition. There are the man-made creations that burn tall into the sky, competing with nature's mountains. These creations are made by fire, dirt and water, and while they may sway in the wind, the wind does not touch them. There are the beautiful people, with fancy machines, fancy clothes, and fancy dwellings. They live in the sky and next to the ocean. They roam the land, manipulating it for their own purposes. From these activities, they eat, breath and create more life in motions of self-sustenance. It is a world of global interaction and interconnection. An overcrowded sphere where each individual is lost in a puddle of humanity.

Yet a movie with only beauty and wonder would be dull and lifeless. So yes, our world has an abundance of scarcity. There are the wastelands of discarded items, the sea of grime flying around a dirty atmosphere, infecting the lungs of the living and the lifeless equally. There are also those individuals in the puddle of humanity who will never know anything fancy, never know anything much at all. Those forgotten people wander through life, unknown to the rest, and not knowing how to represent themselves to the rest. But do not feel sorry or fret for the downtrodden, for they are an essential element in our story.

The third part of the world we are creating is known by all of humanity, but never touched. It is the world of god and angels that watch over the world of the living. These creatures will in all likelihood be around forever, although there is not one among us or them who categorically knows this. But we will assume this to be true, for some aspects of a story require a leap of faith, and this will be ours. But what does this world look like? Well, we will be visiting it later in the story, but for now, let us say that it is neither a happy or sad place. There is no perfection like the rolling hills and fresh streams of our world. But neither is there the abject griminess and unpleasantness that we too often see. And for work and life? Well, these creatures have an indistinguishable link to our world, so one could say that their work is to ensure our two worlds never part.

Now we have three settings for our story to unravel. But what of the smaller details as yet untold, the smell of an individual flower, the sight of a piece of rubbish and the noise of the ocean on a quiet night? These are aspects of the story for you, the reader, to interpret. For while this is the movie of life, each of us will experience the sounds, sights and smells slightly differently.

The movie of life, we could say, is now a place, yet we still know very little about it. We need characters, we need an antagonist, a hero and a heroine, with whom we can enjoy and understand this story. There are three starring roles in this feature.

Our antagonist is from the world of the rich. In fact, our antagonist is not simply one, but it is the power of the world represented through a small group of men (and yes, they must and could only be men). These men run the largest and most powerful parts of the world. They turn the wheel of the economy; they control the advance of technology; and they make the choices of war. Are these men inherently evil? I think not. Yet, they are the cause for what is to come. They are part of the equation that creates the hero, and necessitates the heroine.

The hero comes from the world of the poor for this is the poetic nature of fiction. Yet his movie is not typical of the poor. He is what you might call an enigma – one who comes from the deprived and disenfranchised, but belongs to both the rich and the poor alike. He will save us, and I think you the reader must already realise this. But this is not a story of outcome, it is a story of process. The fact that he will save us is different from seeing how he saves us. But more on his story later.

And finally, our heroine is a beautiful angel. And yes, here again we have a little leap of faith. For the true heroine will always come from heaven, or at least have attributes similar to those found in the wise and beautiful places of the world, the places that take your breath away, the places that remind us that humanity can and will be good and wonderful. They are the antithesis of the antagonist. They are the saviour's saviour. And our heroine is an angel for humanity.

So now our movie of life has its main characters, has its actors who will make the script speak to the audience. These are the people we strive to hate, and try to love. We are now ready, I think, to begin the story that is the movie of life.

In the movie of life our antagonists are sitting in the Organisation of World Society, a place where the world's powerful come together to agree on how to keep the status quo. As we enter this meeting, our antagonists are arguing over the balance of trade, the direction of power and the determination of rules. Only one thing seems clear from these discussions – war is coming.

The world of the antagonists is made up of five major powers and alliances. There is the Eastern Alliance, the Western Coalition, the Southern Formation, the Northern Front and the Central Highlands. Do not fret over remembering all of these, for in essence, they are but five sides of the same square. They are the interpreters of power and the keepers of consistency.

For not a few decades these alliances have operated in a balance of power, each having inherent interests in maintaining the status quo. I have the unpleasant duty however, to inform you that this balance is about to tip.

Our antagonists sit in a room like you might well imagine. It has leather armchairs surrounding a dark timber conference table. The room itself has elements of dark wood, combined with old paintings from a generation long forgotten. There are two doors, one at either end, although most in this room only know where the main entry door leads. Behind the five leaders are the sycophantic advisors, sitting in uncomfortable chairs, notepads on their laps, pens ready to fill up the pages. As they came into the main chamber of the Organisation of World Society, many of our antagonists know that war is more likely than not. But there is still hope it can be prevented.

A tall, elegant man, the leader of the Western Coalition, was the first to take the floor. From his seat, he begins, "My fellow members of this organisation, I appreciate your presence here today. I took it upon myself to get us together to discuss what must be discussed. War looks apparent, but we have it in our power to stop it.

Therefore, I urge us all to look for areas of agreement, not disagreement. We must look towards the strength that has held the world at peace for so long. My Coalition is built on peace, and that is our genuine aim. Yet I must be blunt and say that the Western Coalition cannot and will not stand by and allow others to dictate unfair and unrealistic terms for peace. We all remain prosperous together, or we choose together to fail. I am here today to present a resolution for your consideration. It is an agreement to maintain the peace, to maintain the status quo. There will necessarily be changes to our engagement, but all must give up something to gain peace. Colleagues, the Western Coalition seeks peace and prosperity for all." The leader abruptly stopped, the room unreadable.

The Northern Front leader, a slightly overweight man with a full black beard, took to the floor. "While we appreciate that our Western Coalition friend wishes for peace, he seems intent on war through contradictory actions. I have seen his forces move into position. I have seen his war posturing. If he was serious about maintaining the world's prosperity, then why have propose a ludicrous resolution that gives the Western Coalition further power? I ask, do you all plan to succumb to this hypocrisy? Do you all plan to give up your sovereignty to this megalomaniac? No sir, we do not agree." With that, the Northern Front leader stopped, a hardened look on his already stern face.

A short man with a fancy moustache, the leader of the Southern Formation, was next to speak, "I thank the two gentlemen for their statements. There are now two different versions of events before us. We in the Southern Formation have no great respect for the Western Coalition. But we are seriously concerned that the world is rushing recklessly towards war. We in the Southern Front agree that things must change. But we also agree that today's resolution is indeed absurd and patronising. We are keen to look for ways to find an outcome that will ensure a fairer world with more representation. This will only happen through direct leadership and with a strong vision. I urge all members to find a peaceful outcome to this situation." The man looked expectedly around the room but saw no support in his fellow leaders. He slumped back in his chair.

The Central Highlands leader, a man with a long nose and equally long braided hair, decided it was time to weigh in on this debate. "We would support this resolution with a few small amendments which would strengthen its resolve to push for peace. Like previous colleagues, we question the intention of the Western Coalition, but we are equally sceptical that the rest of you have purer intentions. It is no secret that we are the smallest and weakest of the five powers. We have much to gain from peace. But know that if we head to war, the Central Highlands will never surrender and never rest until we are again the strongest power in the world." The leader paused, and was about to continue when he noticed the leader of the Eastern Alliance sitting up, ready to speak. Reluctantly, the leader yielded to the stronger power.

All faces in the room looked at the Eastern Alliance leader. The man looked more like a gentle doddering grandfather rather than the smart and calculating leader of the second most powerful alliance, after the Western Coalition. But appearances are often deceiving. Everyone in the room, leaders and advisors alike, knew this debate would be decided by how the Eastern Alliance responded. The Eastern Alliance leader's light and thoughtful voice began, "My friends, this is indeed an unfortunate position that we have found ourselves in." A small pause. "While some of you will support our decision, and others will be disappointed in it, we do not consider that we have even made a decision. Rather this decision was made by us all many years ago. This is the inevitable outcome of decades of decisions." The Eastern Alliance leader paused for longer than usual. It was so long that many around the room, had they not known him better, would have thought he was finished. He continued, "We will never support this resolution." The atmosphere in the room suddenly became restless. "And for that reason, we find ourselves at odds with you all." With that, the Eastern Alliance leader stood up, turned on his heels and left, his advisors scrambling in their rush to follow him. Everyone in the room that day would remember this moment. They were at war.

In the movie of his life, our hero is playing football with his best friend. For this is the normality of our hero. He is an ordinary man who takes up a burden and becomes a hero.

Our hero's name is Isaac. While the name itself has religious undertones, his name was chosen at random by his parents. Isaac started out in life at the lower end of the socio-economic spectrum. But through his sheer capability and intelligence, it was not long before others began to notice him. Isaac eventually joined a profession so far removed from his upbringing that his parents, while proud, could not relate to it.

Isaac was exceedingly smart. Academically he succeeded where many failed. He was as beautiful as he was smart, with classically dashing features and an athletic body that had all the girls fawning. Isaac was of course flawed. He was overly ambitious and at times, too impatient. Yet, these flaws were counter-balanced by his friendly nature and a concern for the people he met and the world in which he lived. Isaac was a leader.

After graduating from school, Isaac was able to attend a very prestigious university, a rare opportunity for those that come from the bottom of society. It was there that Isaac met Claire, his future wife and mother of his only child. Claire had come from a well to do family. She worked hard at her studies and eventually became a doctor. Her compassion and intellect were matched only by her beauty. Claire was the most wonderful person Isaac had ever met and together they made a talented couple. It was clear to those who knew them that those two would do great things. It was at university that a certain lecturer of Isaac's (his name is lost to the winds of time) introduced to him the idea of a life of diplomacy.

Upon entering the diplomatic core, Isaac once again shone, outdoing his peers and impressing his seniors. As a diplomat for the Organisation of World Society (he was sent there by the Western Coalition), Isaac had unfettered access to the system. He understood the intricacies of the fragile alliances that held the world together, and he understood how easily they could be broken. As war broke out (in fact it was many wars and skirmishes between shifting power alliances) Isaac was able to traverse the inner workings of the world powers. Through his travels, Isaac would come to discover something. He discovered that war is both necessary and preventable. On this seemingly contradictory concept, we shall return later.

Back to our story. Isaac was playing football in his backyard with his best friend Eric.

"Hey man, you know we never see you around these parts anymore. Too busy with work to visit the neighbourhood?" Eric said.

"I'm sorry, work is pretty hectic lately," Isaac replied. "I am competing with guys whose grandfathers started the Organisation of World Society and I have to work long hours to get noticed."

"Why do you have to be noticed?" Eric asked. Isaac was getting more questions like this from his old friends. They didn't understand his drive, his determination, and especially his conviction that the world teetered on the brink of destruction. He answered, "Because I want to keep playing football with you and I want our children to play football too. Because I'm in a unique position where I'm privy to top-secret information about the world's most powerful groups but I also know what it's like to be at the bottom of the ladder. I know this sounds crazy, but I feel like something drastic needs to be done to stamp out the corruption and greed of the current governments and restore the world to the people. We need a revolution."

Eric looked at his friend and asked a simple question, "Are you sure you want that?"

Isaac replied, "I think so. At the very least I want to help to bring change, and not just sit on the sidelines my whole life."

Eric had been Isaac's best friend during high school. After Isaac went off to university, Eric did a plumbing apprenticeship. After finishing he got a job working for a small company, and he enjoyed his work. Growing up, Eric had never imagined himself, or anyone he knew, living a grander life than what their small town could offer. Looking at his best friend, Eric knew that Isaac was special. Eric spoke again, "Hey man, I don't really understand what you do or how do you it, but I do know that if there's one person who can lead a revolution, it's you."

That night as Isaac lay in bed he thought about what Eric had said earlier, and came to a decision. He was going to have to tread carefully though. A plan like his could easily derail at this stage from any number of mishaps. He would continue to act exactly as expected. But when the strike came, the movie of life would be changed forever.

Isaac arrived at a small airfield located in a town caught between the Western Coalition and the Northern Front. "How long until we arrive at the site?" Isaac asked his host.

"Five minutes sir," came the soldier's response. Isaac had been sent to this town to inspect rumours of a mass grave and report back on who was responsible. This was a sensitive mission and it was less about the truth as it was about the perception of truth. Isaac was chosen for the mission because he was reliable.

Five minutes later Isaac came to the end of the narrow path and was met by a young man with sharp eyes and an attitude. Isaac had the impression he was a conscript rather than a volunteer. It was not unusual these days for whole conscripted units to be operating in hellholes like this. Looking at the captain's insignia pinned to the shoulder of his green uniform, it was clear this young man was in charge. The captain barely glanced at Isaac's paperwork before pointing him in the direction of the site. Isaac heard the captain whispering to one of his soldiers as he walked away, "See private, just another shirt come to decide who should be made responsible for this mess. He's probably likely to go and create another mess somewhere else before the day is out."

Both men could have been court marshalled for such a comment. Unfortunately, thought Isaac, the soldier wasn't wrong.

Isaac found the site. Two enormous holes were filled

with the bodies of men, women and children that had been unceremoniously dumped and cruelly abandoned. Why and how this could occur Isaac did not, and would never, know. But it had occurred and now it was his job to assign responsibility. Isaac thought about his conversation with Eric about leading a revolution, and wondered if this mission would hinder his ability to lead one. By keeping silent he was tacitly consenting to these heinous acts committed by the very people who cared so little for the world for which they were in charge. It was so easy for him to speak of revolution but he didn't even know where to begin to act on that ambition. Isaac headed away from the site, unable to stare any longer into the empty eyes of the dead.

"Captain, how long ago did you find this site?" Isaac asked.

"Two days ago sir," the captain replied.

"And you have not touched or changed anything?" Isaac enquired. The captain stiffened with indignation but he replied courteously, "Of course not sir, we only secured the site against prying eyes and local beasts, as per our orders."

Isaac had seen enough, the event that occurred here was clearly a war crime committed by one of the major alliances. However his report only stated, "Crime committed by local rebellious forces, not in control of either the Western Coalition or the Northern Front." That was the day that Isaac's movie of life was tainted by a crime that was so inhuman, it could only have been committed by humans.

In the movie of life, we are yet to meet our heroine. Our heroine is an angel of great courage, compassion and beauty. She is called Abdiel. At this particular moment, she is weeping quietly as she watches this stage of humanity unfolding below her. War was taking too many lives.

It would be difficult to describe in great detail what Abdiel's world looks, smells or sounds like. It is clean, wondrous, and benign. It is full of the good, and none of the bad. Beyond that, it is difficult for a human mind to conceptualise such a place. The angels who live in that world are kept busy with matters concerning humanity, whether it is watching, discussing or at times interfering. It is of this latter effort that our story will take us. But before Abdiel interferes in the world, she converses with her friend and mentor Ithuriel.

"Ithuriel, their world is collapsing on itself," Abdiel said.

"My dear one, you are too sensitive to their plight. These humans have an uncanny way of bringing themselves out of their own misery at the last moment. It's almost like they do it for sport, were it not so sporadic," Ithuriel replied. He was concerned about Abdiel. She was too anxious about this situation of the humans. Ithuriel was older than Abdiel. Contrary to human beliefs, angels do not live forever, although they do live for an awfully long time. We do not know where or how angels came into existence, only that they are here.

"Abdiel, one day you will mentor young angels like yourself, and you will tell them of this moment. And with firsthand knowledge you will be able to tell them that humans always recover and will continue to prosper, expand and develop all on their own."

Abdiel replied, "That might be true Ithuriel, however I don't know if I can just sit here now and do nothing."

"Abdiel, let me tell you about other angels that have interfered with the world of the humans. Do you know of Zephon the messenger? One day Zephon was sitting and watching the humans kill one another and thought to himself, they will kill each other until there is none left. So without a plan and without discussing it with others, Zephon decided to involve himself in their war. He picked a side and helped tip the balance in their favour. They won the war. What happened next he did not expect. The victors pursued and killed every man, woman and child who were allied to the side who had fought against them. It was then that Zephon realised he would never really understand humans and that interfering had been a mistake. His interfering cost more lives, lives that might have lived on had he used more brain and less emotion."

Ithuriel looked at Abdiel. She was so young and had so much potential. She was both compassionate and intelligent, which was a powerful combination when mixed with wisdom and age. Abdiel knew the story of Zephon. She knew Ithuriel was right, and she also knew there was no need to share her thoughts with him on this subject of interfering with the humans. Abdiel was beginning to form a plan. Of this, we shall learn more later on.

In this movie of life, our antagonists are at war. So far we know little of their strategy, little of their motives, other than a keen desire to remain in power. But let us be clear, power for them is not for power's sake. Rather, they believe they are protecting humanity from the blight of one of the other powers. This is a war of ideology.

At this point in our story the leader of the Western Coalition is discussing the war with a certain general, a man who was the head of the army and a trusted advisor.

"Tell me how the war is progressing."

The general saluted and in a confident voice answered, "The Northern Front seems to be in retreat sir, but we just received word that the Southern Formation has launched an attack on one of our bases."

The leader considered this and, leaning back on his chair, asked, "Are you confident of decisive victory?"

"Yes sir," replied the general without hesitation. "Even accounting for our losses there is no doubt that our armies will prevail. This foolish attack by the Southern Front will not set us back as they are also caught up in a skirmish with the Central Highlands, and their forces are stretched too thin. We will push them back in a matter of days."

"Thank you. Dismissed." The leader waved him out of

the room.

From a side door the leader's closest advisor entered the room. Jom was a man of little character, a classic villain. He was thin, with greasy black hair, and most people loathed him from the moment they met him. "Jom," the leader said, "what are your thoughts on our strategy and the grand plan?" It was the question the leader of the Western Coalition asked most often, and Jom was becoming adept at answering it. In his oily voice Jom replied, "It appears to me sir, that we must keep the Eastern Alliance busy. They are our biggest threat. Now that our war with the Northern Front has ended we should encourage them to attack the Eastern Alliance to distract both powers from focusing on us."

The leader thought for a moment. "And how would you entice the Northern Front to make war on the Eastern Alliance?"

Looking flustered Jom replied, "Sir, it's best if I don't say, for then you will be able to speak the truth when asked that you knew nothing about how the war started."

"Yes, you are quite right. But tell me, are we winning the ideological war? For this is the real war. We need to convince the world populations that we stand for freedom and justice above all other governments."

Jom thought for a moment before replying, "We are not losing that war sir. We will keep up the pressure on the propaganda and we will win the hearts and minds of the people." Satisfied with how things were progressing, the leader dismissed Jom.

Abdiel watched humanity and formulated her plan. She had identified her target and knew that she couldn't ignore the humans who were crying out for help any longer. Abdiel took to the sky, soaring on the winds of destiny, and flew down to earth for the first time. She disguised herself as a richly dressed middle aged woman and followed her target into a bar that was half full of people. She introduced herself and they talked for hours. The target knew that Abdiel was more than what she claimed. Her ideas were dangerous, more than that, treasonous. But she was not wrong either. Abdiel could see that her target was almost convinced. She asked one more question. "Do you want to create a future or let others create it for you?" Abdiel left after that. Her target was deep in thought. He hadn't really needed convincing, he just lacked the courage before now to take action. The strange woman had pointed out to him that courage is always within you, and you can choose to ignore it or use it as you wish. The target left the bar and walked in the direction of the particular city described by Abdiel, walked in the direction of our hero Isaac. Along the way, the target spoke with many people. He listened to them describe acts of horror committed by the world powers. He was learning about the world from a bigger perspective. He was seeing the damage done by those in power, and more importantly, to those without power.

In this movie of life, Isaac is in the major city of the Southern Formation, gathering information about the war. At this point Isaac is finishing a meeting with the Southern Formation Ministry of Peace. In his calm and collected manner he is speaking with officials trained in the art of deception. But his parents taught Isaac well and his manners hold up even in the face of blatant disrespect.

After the meeting Isaac decided to stop at a local tavern and enjoy a proper meal. While he is eating, Abdiel's target enters the tavern. He has been travelling on foot for days, guided by strange dreams. He instinctively knows who Isaac is and walks up to him.

"Hello Isaac, my name is Jacob and I have a proposition for you."

Let us stop for a moment to consider Jacob. He's one of those side characters that doesn't get credited in a story, but without him there would be no story. Not classically handsome, with brown hair and an average build, Jacob is not the wittiest person around but he is sharp enough, and people enjoy having him around. We will learn more about Jacob as the story progresses, but here Jacob is Isaac's courage. He is that voice in your head telling you to make the leap of faith, to take that chance in life. He is optimism and pragmatism personified.

Isaac assumed the man had been sent by the Southern Formation but it was clear after his first comment that this man wanted something entirely different.

"You want to start a revolution."

Isaac gaped at the man's knowledge, but Jacob continued without pause, "As you already know, this war is about ensuring the power of the current governments and not about the true needs of their peoples. I had a visit from a woman who was not from this world. I know that sounds crazy but she told me that you, and only you, can build the foundations for a new kind of world. Your revolution could create a world in which equality, fairness and justice are not just catchphrases but realities, in which poverty, disease and tyranny become distant memories. This woman told me that you will help us make a better future".

Isaac was sceptical, as anyone would be. But Isaac was always taught not to dismiss impossible or crazy ideas for they heralded the seeds of change. So he asked a practical question. "How would I lead people?"

Jacob heard Isaac's doubting tone and replied, "You provide a symbol and I find you the opportunity to give a moving speech to reach the people who will help you change the world. I have already begun to build you an organisation, with chapters in the many towns I passed through on my way to find you. There is genuine excitement and hope that things can change, that there is someone with the ability and knowledge to make it happen. The people just need a leader and they will follow."

Jacob could see that Isaac was not so easily convinced and Abdiel had warned him of this possibility. Jacob therefore simply said, "There is nothing you need do at this stage. I will continue my work until you are ready to lead us." With that, Jacob got up and walked away. Isaac sat back in his chair, drink in hand, thinking about this strange conversation. He looked around wondering if anyone else had heard Jacob. What he had said was nearly treasonous. Should he report it? What if Jacob was telling the truth? Did he really want to stifle a possible revolution that he would, in all probability, support? Could Isaac actually lead such a revolution? And would he want to?

In this movie of life the angel Abdiel watched the stories of Isaac and Jacob cross over and create ripples with unseen consequences. Abdiel saw that she had chosen well in Jacob. He was smart, energetic and able to speak to people. People trusted him easily. Abdiel watched as Jacob traversed the globe, accepting gifts of food from people and finding ingenious ways to travel cheaply. After only six months Jacob had started a movement that was gaining a name and a reputation. But it still needed a leader. Abdiel even considered that perhaps Jacob was that leader, but he never showed any interest in leading, telling people that the leader would reveal himself at the right moment. Abdiel also watched Isaac with interest. At first he had seemed uninterested in the idea of change, but after a few months of his apparent disinterest, Isaac began putting out small feelers. In towns and cities he would visit as part of his job, he would ask people about an organisation trying to overthrow the world powers. Most people at first claimed not to know of any such organisation, but after some clever coaxing by Isaac every person he asked would answer that they had heard of it. Some would venture to say they were a member, or the local leader. After six months however, Abdiel realised Isaac was not moving fast enough in his acceptance of this organisation, so she decided to make one last intervention. And so our hero and heroine finally met.

On this fateful day Isaac was in a small town outside of a major city in the territory of the Eastern Alliance. He was eating in a local restaurant quietly thinking to himself.

"Good evening Isaac."

Isaac looked up. He had not noticed anyone enter the restaurant. A lady was standing in front of him, not so much beautiful as radiating a glow that lit up her features.

"I will not take up too much of your time. I am the one

Jacob spoke of when you met. I am here to give you one simple message. Stop thinking about leading and begin leading the organisation. They need you."

Isaac was unsure what to think and he had many questions he wanted to ask, but before he could speak Abdiel continued, "When you spoke with your best friend Eric, you knew within yourself that one day you would lead, and so did he."

There was no way anyone this far from his home could have known about Eric, let alone the nature of their private conversation. Isaac looked down at his food confused, and then up again to confront her, but the lady had disappeared. Remembering Jacob's words about a mysterious woman, Isaac again wondered, just for a second, whether he could in fact lead a revolution.

And a second was all Abdiel needed. She had successfully planted the seed of possibility into his mind.

In the movie of life Jacob is discussing guerrilla tactics with his spymaster Marko. Marko is a quiet and patient man. Marko is neither handsome nor unattractive but has one of those unremarkable faces that you could not pick out of a crowd. His intellect and past experience (a mystery to all in the organisation except a chosen few) ensured his rise to prominence within the rebel organisation. Those few who meet him find him detached and at times borderline rude, but his loyalty to the cause was without question.

Marko and Jacob were conversing in an empty office at the rebel headquarters.

"We need to increase our presence around the world," Marko remarked, "It's time for us to expand our reach and create global attention, grab global headlines and step up recruitment." Jacob looked up from his paperwork. He hadn't realised when he took on his role as deputy leader how much paperwork he would be in charge of. Jacob and Marko had never entirely trusted one another, but they respected each other's different yet complementary skill sets. Jacob responded lightly, "We are making the moves we have been ordered to make. You know that we need to play this smart, even if it takes slightly longer."

With visible frustration Marko continued his argument, "You and Isaac are wrong Jacob, the five powers will last longer than we could ever hope to, and without decisive action our own people will desert us or turn on each other. Our governments can afford to wait out this unrest until we eventually implode and fail in our mission. Have you spoken to Isaac about our next steps?"

"No, but he keeps telling me he wants to go public," Jacob replied. Marko thought about this for a moment and said, "Maybe that's not such a bad idea. He's across all of the news waves as the spokesperson for the Organisation of World Society. His announcement as the leader of our organisation would be the perfect opportunity to alert the world to our presence."

Jacob replied, "We will lose control of the process Marko. Once Isaac is public, we lose the surprise element and instantly raise the stakes."

"Exactly Jacob," Marko responded, "We need this publicity or we start to lose momentum."

Jacob trusted Marko when it came to strategy. Jacob had almost single-handedly started this rebellion but he suspected that Marko was the right man to finish the job. Together, the two men had successfully built up Isaac as a man of the people, without actually letting the people know who Isaac was. With this in mind, Jacob looked up and replied, "I can see your point, and as always, value your counsel. I will talk to Isaac this evening and if he agrees we can go public in one week. I trust you will be able to make the necessary arrangements."

Marko replied, "Thank you. I will provide you details in time for your meeting with Isaac. I would also like to attend your meeting so that I can answer any questions Isaac may have."

Jacob simply nodded.

In the movie of life, Ithuriel was sure that Abdiel had interfered in the human world, and was on his way to speak with her about it. He had been watching, and saw the extraordinary rise of the rebel organisation. He came upon her and looked around to make sure they were alone.

"Abdiel, what have you done?" Ithuriel asked. "I warned you not to interfere with humans. Their world and the way they think is very different from our world and our rules. You must allow them to go through life as they need."

"Are you finished scolding me?" Abdiel snapped. "Yes, I interfered, and now there is a revolution. I disagree with you Ithuriel; I believe we are meant to interfere, but only if the final choices are always made by human. But we can help them to see all the possibilities that they might miss."

Ithuriel considered Abdiel. He had always thought of her, as the humans put it, as a younger sister. And now, like many siblings, they were fighting. Of course, neither would admit how human they were acting at this stage.

"Abdiel, I cannot agree with you on this point. It is not our destiny to engage in the short lives of these humans. There will be generations more, and they shall ever continue."

Abdiel looked directly into Ithuriel's eyes. "We shall see," she said, and walked away.

While many consider angels to be superior to humans (if they consider the existence of angels at all, but if pressed would likely defer to this widely-held belief), however they are in fact just different versions of the same type of being, like two sides of the same coin. But an angel's perception of the human world is different to a human's simply because of their long life. Ithuriel wondered what to do next. It was an unwritten rule in their world that one did not involve oneself in the folly of humanity. Ithuriel knew the elders wouldn't approve of Abdiel's actions, but in order to protect his friend he decided to keep the matter quiet for now and attempt to correct the mistake himself. His decision made, Ithuriel travelled down to the human world to visit the Western Coalition leader. This, Ithuriel decided, would rebalance the scales Abdiel had upset. "Mr Chairman, you are the leader of the greatest alliance in this world. Would you like to know who is in charge of this so-called revolution, and how to stop them?" As you can imagine, the leader was indeed interested in hearing more. Of this conversation, I will leave to your imagination. Needless to say the leader was sufficiently convinced.

In the movie, our hero Isaac takes a short trip home. Isaac had decided to seek guidance from his friend Eric. "It's amazing," Isaac excitedly said to him when they were alone. "We are on the verge of officially starting this revolution. At the beginning I was sceptical, but now I think we might actually have a chance at changing the world."

Eric looked at his best friend, thinking how far Isaac had come. He answered, "You have done an amazing thing, and you can't stop now, you must complete what you have started."

Isaac replied, "Thanks for your support. But I want to ask you something. I trust your advice and your judgement. I need someone who can be my extra eyes and ears in meetings. I need someone to tell me the truth so that I can be sure I am making the right decisions. The problem with living a double life is that you never know who you can trust. I want you to come back with me and be a part of our organisation. Will you do this for me?"

"Isaac it seems to me that you are already making all of the right decisions, and it's well known that you have amazing advisors." Eric paused, before cautiously asking, "Do the five powers know that you are the leader?"

"No, not yet," Isaac replied, "But Marko is working out the details for a public announcement next week. He feels that we can use it to undermine the powers, given my public role with their society." Isaac looked over towards his security detail. Given Isaac's importance to the great powers, they had agreed to provide him with a security detail. What they didn't know was that these men had actually joined the revolution. Sometimes Isaac felt responsible for so many people that it almost entirely consumed him. After everything that had happened, all the risks he had taken, he still cared about people, about individuals.

Eric watched his best friend struggling under the weight

of responsibility. He made a decision. "I will come with you. But I must not have a high ranking role. I will be a lowly assistant, helping with your schedule, listening to conversations. It's safer for you, and me, that way. Deal?"

Isaac replied, "Deal. You had better pack. This is going to be an adventure."

In the movie of life, Isaac's wife and life partner Claire is eating lunch with their daughter. We have not really seen much of Isaac's family during this story. Claire is a very supportive wife. She loves Isaac. She knows what he does and has been part of every decision he has made. She remembers well the night Isaac came home after visiting a mass grave. She recalls vividly how Isaac shook as he sobbed in her arms. She knew Isaac wanted to do more, she knew he would do more, and she knew right now he needed her support. So she supported him, all the while raising their intelligent, beautiful and kind daughter.

When Isaac had returned home after his first meeting with Abdiel, he had stayed up all night talking with Claire, making decisions about the next steps. Getting

Eric to work with and watch over Isaac was part of Claire's plan. She knew the risks, the sacrifices that would have to be made. But more than that, she understood the scope of what Isaac was attempting and what he was affecting.

"Mummy, are you okay?"

Claire looked down at her daughter, realising that she had stopped talking mid-sentence, lost in reverie. "Yes darling, sorry. As I was saying, your father is doing amazing work which is why we do not see him as often as other children see their fathers. But I want you to know something. He loves you very much even though he has very important work to do. One day your father will change the world."

In the movie of life, the leaders of both the Southern Formation and the Northern Front have met on neutral territory and are discussing the growing threat from the terrorist organisation and how best to eliminate it. At this point in time these two powers are not at war with one another, but instead have temporarily allied because they have the same enemies.

"The Northern Front is the natural ally of the Southern

Formation, because of both the growing terrorist organisation and the prevailing threat posed by the other arrogant powers," said the leader of the Northern Front. The two men were sitting opposite each other on comfortable leather armchairs, aperitif in hand. They had left their sycophants in the adjoining room, who were no doubt comparing their levels of importance and influence.

The leader of the Southern Formation responded, a serious look on his wrinkled face, "Yes I agree that we are natural allies, and I would be happy to form an arrangement against the other powers. I know that we could break the dominance of the allied Eastern Front and Western Coalition. I am also willing to create an alliance against this terrorist organisation, although if we are going to speak frankly, let us speak of this organisation as a revolutionary force. They are not just set upon causing global fear and anarchy, they have a purpose, one which is dedicated to changing the nature of global power. They continue to pose a serious threat which must be crushed."

The leader of the Northern Front, a man who had little sympathy for anyone, smiled and said, "Yes, they are no terrorist organisation. We have funded terrorist organisations, and this revolutionary force, as you say, is much more problematic in their idealism. We must eliminate them before they gain too much popular support. Maybe we could use them for our own ends, and get them labelled as terrorists?" he mused.

"Then we'll start by announcing that Isaac is the leader of this terrorist organisation. It should be known that the Western Coalition's man is the one leading this disruptive organisation." The Southern Formation leader paused, letting this new information sink in. The fact that Isaac was the leader of this uprising was something he had only found out this morning. The stunned Northern Front leader replied, "Are you sure? Isaac is our global spokesperson. This is a man whom we have all supported and whose loyalty was never questioned! We will be on the symbolic defensive. Our ignorance speaks volumes in this matter."

"You worry too easily," replied the Southern Formation leader, "Everything is prepared. I have produced a negative advertising campaign to discredit Isaac and all our news agencies will increase their focus on this terrorist organisation, and its negative impacts. We will crush them with illegitimacy."

The Northern Front leader was a shrewd and tactical man and saw his chance to use Isaac's terrorist organisation to discredit all the other powers. "Yes," he thought, "this is an opportunity." And to his Southern Formation counterpart he raised his glass in salute.

In the movie of life, Marko, the spymaster of Global Spring (which is the name of Isaac's organisation) was sitting at his desk working on plans for expansion of the organisation. He had spent all night considering the current political situation. He knew that Isaac's role as leader needed to be made public. He also knew that it needed to happen on his terms, in the right way. This was why Marko had sent one of his spies to the Southern Formation to tell the leader there about Isaac's true identity.

Reading through the notes on the recent meeting between the leaders of the Southern Formation and the Northern Front, Marko smiled at the discussion that had taken place. By all accounts the leaders had accepted that Global Spring was a threat to their existence.

Marko often spent nights at his desk. With no partner, children or family, there was nothing waiting at home for him. Marko lived for the job. He lived for the information, for the knowledge pouring in from around the world and around the clock thanks to his operatives. At one stage Marko thought he might want to lead this revolution himself, but then he realised two things. Firstly, there was great power in a global network of information. Leaders, Marko surmised, were far more liable to political change than those behind the scenes in charge of the information. And secondly, Marko knew he was not a leader. The power would go to his head and he would eventually fail. That is why he had supported Isaac. He knew Isaac had always been a reluctant leader, and he had good, if idealistic, intentions. All of this was why Marko was content just to follow.

Marko knew it was the team that kept the revolution moving forward, everyone had a role to play. Marko knew his value and enjoyed his role, and he was given a large amount of autonomy to get the job done. He suspected Jacob and Isaac knew that he did things they would not support, but they never asked about anything apart from what they needed to know.

Marko put the final touches on the documentation that he had been working on all night, a plan to form Global Spring's military force, which he had called the Global Army. It was structured like all modern armies, and was formed primarily from the armed militias and spies that had done much of Marko's, and Global Spring's, dirty work. The formation of an army was just one more step in his wider vision to overthrow the great powers. Marko now moved on to the next stage of his planning, how to win this war.

 In the movie of life, the leader of the Western Coalition is sitting at his desk, scheming and planning. His desk is modern, with modern utilities, rather than the somewhat nostalgic, dated styles of the other world powers. The man himself is your typical villain, brilliant, ruthless, and flawed. This leader is the head of the largest of the world's military forces and is in the middle of planning the invasion of the Southern Formation. He is also planning a strategic defence, using part of his vast resources to protect the Western Coalition's borders, especially from its strongest threat, the Eastern Alliance. The Western Coalition leader however is not taking into consideration the ragtag terrorist organisation that has consumed so much time of the other leaders' time. He thinks the organisation has been created by one of the other leaders in order to further their own ambitions.

"I think you really should take more notice of this

terrorist organisation," a voice suddenly said, startling the leader. He remembered locking his office so that he would not be disturbed, so how had this stranger suddenly appeared, as if out of nowhere?

"That terrorist organisation is not a threat created by another world power, it is a real threat to you," the mellifluous voice continued. Recovering from the shock of the intruder, the leader grabbed the weapon hidden under his desk and pointed it casually at the strange looking man before him. "And you are?" he asked in his most commanding voice.

"My name is Ithuriel and I am here to save your Coalition and remove this terrorist threat." The man was very beautiful, radiant and strong. The Western Coalition leader looked him up and down, noting he was wearing few clothes to show off his perfectly toned chest. "How did you get in here?" he demanded.

"I appeared," was the curt reply. "But what is more important," angel continued, "is why I am here and how I can help you."

"How can you help me?"

The reply came swiftly, "The man known as Isaac, your spokesperson, is the leader of this terrorist organisation. He is your enemy."

The leader was not one to pass up an opportunity, even

if it did seem strange. In an attempt to demonstrate that he was in charge the leader said, "You have my attention. Now, would you care for a drink?"

"No, where we come from, your form of drink provides no comfort, but please, feel free to have one yourself."

This man, or whatever he was, might be strange but the leader was not so arrogant as to believe refusing his help might not have dire consequences. He had found in his life that it was best not to ask questions that would lead to an answer one might not want to hear. And so the two sat for the next hour formulating a plan.

Later, the Western Coalition leader would call his closest advisors into his office and show them the new plans that had come from his discussion with Ithuriel. For all his wisdom, Ithuriel had given too much in haste, and thus tipped the scales in unpredictable ways.

In the movie of life our fearless hero Isaac is preparing to give his first speech as the leader of Global Spring. In the space of a week, Isaac was denounced by the five powers as the traitorous leader of a terrorist organisation, declared rogue and a bounty was placed on his head. Marko was forced to use his newly created

Global Army to keep the organisation from being destroyed completely. The world is now is a state of civil war, with Global Spring fighting against the world powers, amidst the battles still raging between the powers. Global Spring grew exponentially, its army doubling in size as Marko predicted. It was all moving along very fast

Waiting by the side of the outdoor stage, Isaac watched the thousand people who had gathered. His speech was to be broadcasted to the world. It was to be the rallying cry to the Global Army troops. Isaac was announced and entered the stage to raucous applause.

"There was a time in history when our humanity brought forth in this world a new type of ideal. An ideal that was conceived in freedom and dedicated to the proposition that all on earth are born, and shall always be, equal. Now we are engaged in a war of ideals, a war to test this proposition. It is a war we must win, for only then can we be free to build communities of united individuals, not apparatuses of power. The world must take note, not of what we say here; but of what we do here.

"Today, I announce to the world that Global Spring will win this war. We will win because we believe in the equality of people, in the inherent and indisputable right to our freedom. I am just one person who helped form Global Spring, but if we are united we will win this war in the name of people everywhere.

"Global Spring was formed as a peaceful organisation. An organisation dedicated to helping communities, correcting injustices, and most importantly, giving hope to those who have abandoned hope. A better world is needed. A better system is required.

"We tried all lawful modes of expressing opposition, of expressing change. And each time we used the system, the doors of change in the system were closed one by one because of those in power. We are forced into a situation in which we either accept that we would never be free, or we defy the world powers. We chose to defy the law. We chose to represent the people.

"When our peaceful organisation was seen as a threat and the world powers resorted to a show of force, we have answered their violence with our own strength. We still believe in diplomacy as a means of solving any disputes, but this is not the reality of our enemy. We realized that in order to create our vision of a better world, we may have to face the prospect of a civil or even a global war. But know that this is our last resort. We did not want to be committed to war, but we are ready to face any challenge.

"Global Spring has been denounced as a terrorist organisation. We have been denounced by unjust laws, designed to keep you from ever questioning those in power. And for no greater reason than those in power want to keep on being powerful. They do not care about your lives. The truth is those in power must serve the people, and if they do not serve them, they must answer to the people.

"We have before us many long months of struggle and pain. Our aim is to wage war by sea, land and air, with all the strength that god can give us; to wage war against immense tyranny. Our goal is victory, for without victory, there is no survival. Either we win, or they will crush us all. Those in power will destroy every man, woman and child. We deserve more. We deserve freedom. And it is for our freedom that we fight and win!

"Let us go forward together with our united strength. Let us decide to take back our freedom. Let us change the world!"

With this, Isaac left the stage. He left behind him a world not just ready for war, but hungry for change.

In the movie of life, Abdiel sat in her realm, watching

the human circus unfold. She watched Marko directing his army and was impressed; she watched Isaac speak to his people and was inspired; and she watched Ithuriel meet the leader of the Western Coalition and was dismayed. It was this last act in particular, she realised, which would change the whole movie of life. While Abdiel had indeed interfered, she had only whispered, as was the way of angels. Ithuriel by comparison had directly shared information, had given away secrets that would alter the course of humanity. Even with the best intentions, there was a difference between inspiring humans to be the best version of themselves, and manipulating them.

While Ithuriel was more senior than Abdiel, she knew she was obligated to report his activities. History has not recorded the name of the angel Abdiel met with. History cannot even confirm if the angel was male or female, or a different creation altogether. Sufficient to say that this angel is old, ancient even, and far more powerful that either Abdiel or Ithuriel. Abdiel entered the realm of this ancient angel, knelt and bowed her head, and began the necessary formalities.

"Thank you for breaking your silence to meet with me today".

The angel replied, "Abdiel, the angel that cares, has not

yet made her final decision." These ancient beings often spoke in riddles and incomplete sentences. Abdiel continued, "I watched the human wars and interfered. I inspired two humans to begin their rebellion. I only guided, as many of my forebears have also done." Abdiel paused, briefly looking up, but the ancient angel only looked at her, passively waiting for her to continue.

Abdiel said, "The angel Ithuriel bade me not to interfere, and while I did not adhere to his advice, I was careful. Ithuriel in turn interfered on the pretext of balancing my actions, but he did not guide or encourage. He has provided information to the humans that will change the course of the war. He has provided them with knowledge enough that they now start to question about our world. I seek your advice." With this, Abdiel once again bowed her head.

The ancient considered Abdiel for a while. The angel had been watching both Ithuriel and Abdiel for many eons now. The angel knew that angels did interfere at times, their own nature would not allow them to ignore what happens on earth. And the current situation on earth presented an opportunity to affect greater change in their own realms. But such a change would require sacrifice by these two angels, even if they did not yet know it.

The angel dismissed Abdiel without further comment and Ithuriel was summoned. Ithuriel was immediately banished from their world and was exiled to earth indefinitely. In despair, Ithuriel left without saying a word. Unbeknownst to him, the ancient angel was gambling with his fate for an outcome which was uncertain. Normally an angel of such wisdom could see many steps ahead, but these were uncertain times and a new world was being formed, one which was worth gambling for.

A shocked a confused Ithuriel fell to earth. But he was now remorseful and wished to correct his wrongs. His extensive knowledge of humanity enabled him to quickly adapt to human life, and although he missed Abdiel fiercely, he never forgot why he was now here.

Abdiel wept as she watched her friend depart for earth for the last time. Had she made a mistake? All she wanted was to rebalance the scales, not destroy her friend's existence as an angel.

How these two angels would affect and change the world were still unknown, but the ancient angel that sent Ithuriel to the realm of humans knew one thing,

Abdiel and Ithuriel still had an important role to play in the movie of life.

In the movie of life, Marko is meeting with a senior member of the Eastern Alliance. Marko realised that to succeed, Global Spring needed to divide the five powers, and he thought that the Eastern Alliance would be the most open to change.

"I want to form a truce with you. We will stop all activity in your lands and you will provide clemency for those involved with our organisation. You will then support us to reform the Organisation of World Society." This was Marko's opening gambit, as he had very little to offer the Eastern Alliance.

The other man considered Marko's offer. He was a reasonably short man, with an alarming smile, and wise eyes. This was a man called king maker by those in the Eastern Alliance. There was no doubt in this man's mind that Marko could do what he said. But given his reputation, he couldn't possibly be trusted.

Sitting opposite Marko in this small café on neutral territory, the senior member of the Eastern Alliance had a few questions. "I am willing to provide clemency for all of the members of your terrorist organisation in our lands, but I see no reason to support you in the Organisation of World Society."

Marko was actually surprised by how quickly this man had agreed to the first of his terms. Marko decided to push a little further. "My friend, your Eastern Alliance is held together through the fear of what might happen if a power vacuum occurred. Your support of the Organisation of World Society will guarantee stability. Furthermore you will change your political system to be more inclusive. Our members would demand no less. In return, we will stop harassing your lands and you will have an opportunity to be the only power left in the world."

The other man's face was unreadable. He decided to remind Marko who still had the power here. The Eastern Alliance was open to a deal, but not at too high a cost. He replied, "You need to stop your activities in our lands. You are running short on resources and your organisation is stretched too thin. I know you are under threat in a number of areas and you want to be free to focus your attention elsewhere."

Marko did not even blink, but did subtly change tack, realising the man was actually serious about a deal. He said, "You are correct. If we are able to come to an agreement, we could leave your lands and focus our resources elsewhere. But this would actually be better for you than for us. You too are under threat from other powers and if we continue to harass you, the Eastern Alliance would have to continue wasting resources fighting us. If we leave, we both have resources to fight the other powers. Together we change the balance of power. Alone the stalemate continues."

The other man smiled. It seemed he had underestimated his opponent. This alliance would be a win for both sides. He decided to take a risk and said, "We will support you in the Organisation of World Society but we will not be held hostage and change our political system. Your people will have clemency but if they choose to live in our land, it will be under our rules."

Marko replied, "I can agree to those terms. I will reach out today and call a halt to activities." The Eastern Alliance leader reached out his hand and shook with Marko. He said, "Then we have a deal. We will begin the process of delisting Global Spring as a terrorist organisation." This had been a remarkably quick negotiation, but both sides knew the cost of inaction, and the advantages of a truce. And neither needed to remind the other what would happen if the deal was not honoured.

In the movie of life, the Western Coalition is in trouble. After descending to earth, Ithuriel regretted his previous errors and decided the people of the Western Coalition deserved a better life. With this in mind he established a following and began a rebellion within the Western Coalition to force change. Ithuriel's forces quickly gained land and more troops. While nominally supporting Global Spring, his little organisation was not officially part of it. The Western Coalition was caught by surprise by Ithuriel's attacks.

"Gentlemen, I have gathered you all here today to deal with the threats we face to our Coalition," began the leader of the Western Coalition. He had gathered all his senior people and brought them into the capital to discuss the threats posed by Isaac and Ithuriel. Sitting in the main boardroom, a panoramic view of the Western Coalition lands behind them, one of the men responded, "Sir, we have lost control, by conservative estimates, of at least twenty percent of our territory, which is now in either Isaac's or Ithuriel's control. At the current rate, one of these groups will reach the capital within the month. While we do not think they are coordinating, it seems Ithuriel has taken great care not to attack any of Isaac's territory, and Isaac has in turn not attacked Ithuriel."

The Western Coalition leader responded, "Can we plan an attack on one of their groups and make it seem like an attack from the other? If we can reduce their forces, we have more of a chance of crushing both of them."

The deputy responded, "We have tried that sir, but it appears as if they have some type of communication and realised that the attack was from us, and not each other."

The leader stood up, facing away from his men and surveying his lands. He considered himself the only person who could bring these lands together, and continue the prosperity to which his country was accustomed. Times were desperate, so the Western Coalition Leader took a gamble and decided to tell the men about his meeting with Ithuriel some months past. He had heard whispers that some of his men were already in secret negotiation with these groups, and he hoped that if they learned the truth it would strengthen their resolve to fight. He said, "This may be hard to believe, but Ithuriel is not quite human, and he fights us with ungodly powers. Surely you have all heard the rumours about that entire fleet which was lost in that unnatural storm. I don't know the extent of his power but I do know that he is not one of us, and therefore has no right to lead men in a war against the legitimate government. He must be destroyed. And we need to make sure that Isaac knows that it was Ithuriel who betrayed him."

"I have already made peace with Ithuriel and have formed an alliance against you."

The Western Coalition leader quickly spun. He heard the voice, but did not want to believe it could be true. The man who had spoken was one of his oldest and most trusted advisors. How could he have signed an alliance with Ithuriel? If it was true, the Western Coalition was lost, as this man controlled lands that provided access to important infrastructure across the country. His lands were also the arms manufacturing heartland of the Western Coalition and its loss would be irreparably harmful to his rule.

He saw resolve, passion and even pride on the face of this traitor. Looking around the room, the other men were either staring at the ground or staring straight in his eyes. It was at this moment that the Western Coalition leader, for the first time, began to doubt he could win this war.

"There is no point calling for your guards. They are all loyal to the protection of the Western Coalition, which now does not include you." The traitor continued, "I will walk out of here safely today, and I will take these other men with me. You are finished. Times change and we cannot continue the outdated ways of the past. I have arranged safe passage for you to a secret location where you can live out the rest of your life in peace."

The Western Coalition leader saw the betrayal, but did to want to believe it. "I will not have your pity. We have been together for many decades, and this is how I am treated in the end?" he screamed. The deputy calmly responded, "There are only two choices sir. Hiding or death. I do not have time to bargain but when I walk out of here I will make the decision for you." The Western Coalition leader blustered and raged but they all turned their backs and walked out. He knew a lost fight when he saw one. Defeated, he went into hiding.

In this movie of life, the world has changed significantly since we first met our hero, heroine and antagonists on page one.

In a very short space of time the Western Coalition fell and Isaac signed a treaty with Ithuriel to take control of those lands. It was split into several self-ruling territories, and was newly named the Western Union. Ithuriel included many of the senior members from the old regime in the new Union, on condition that the land become a beacon of freedom. Ithuriel was head of this Union but the power was distributed between the new territories, who controlled many of the taxes and laws, while the central government controlled defence and international relations. Ithuriel knew that by distributing power, the people would rule the leaders, and not the other way around. Ithuriel was a good leader, having learned from all other human leaders throughout history.

Marko's deal had been successful, and the Global Army had stopped fighting the Eastern Alliance. In quick succession the remaining three powers, weakened from years of fighting, and seeing the greatest empire fallen, signed peace treaties with Global Spring and were forced to give independence to many parts of their countries. What emerged was a number of small but sovereign and free nations. These new nations chose to join a new international organisation established by Isaac. This organisation provided them with a voice and created global norms for all to abide by. The Western Union, led by Ithuriel, also joined this new organisation. Not being given much of a choice, the Eastern Alliance reluctantly joined.

Isaac became the head of the new international organisation, and Global Spring was disbanded. Many of the former members joined the new organisation. Those who had been in the Global Army became the standing army for this new organisation. And while pockets of fighting continued around the world, the world now had a global institutional mechanism that was owned by all and was dedicated to freedom rather than power.

But the movie of life is rarely calm for long.

"Eric, I just need five minutes and then we can head to the ceremony," Isaac told his best friend. Isaac was due to be inaugurated as the first head of the new international organisation. Claire walked in with their daughter in tow and said, "You truly look like a leader. I'm so proud of you." Isaac reached down and picked up his daughter. He looked at his wife and smiled back. "Yes, I think I'm ready for the next stage of this crazy adventure," he replied. Together as a family they walked out of the regal suite on the top floor of the hotel chosen to host the inauguration. Eric escorted the family to the waiting room behind the main hall where Isaac would be presented to the people and leaders of the world. Claire and their daughter gave Isaac one last hug before going out of the room to take their place in the VIP section of the hall.

Claire looked around at the thousands of people crowded into the hall. Aside from seating for the member states of the organisation, it was standing room only. Everyone was squashed together, talking excitedly. "It really is quite a sight."

Claire turned her head and smiled at a grinning Jacob. Marko was behind him, accompanied by a lady Claire had never met. "Yes it is. And I suspect there were very few people who thought this would ever come to pass," Claire replied. Marko leaned forward and over Jacob's shoulder, responded, "This is your night too Claire. You have supported him over these years. We are so proud to have you with us tonight. And they love you. Just look at how many people are looking and waving." Turning, Claire realised that there were people waving and smiling in their direction. She stood up and waved at the crowd and the whole audience cheered and waved back, their jubilation infectious.

"Claire," continued Marko, "Let me introduce you to Abdiel." Abdiel had sought permission to come for this ceremony from her realm. Claire turned and greeted the angel.

"I'm very glad to finally make your acquaintance lady, you were a great influence on my husband," she said.

Abdiel replied, "It was your husband who did the hard work. I simply planted the seed," and she bowed to Claire. Claire heard the audience begin to cheer and she turned around to see her husband coming up to the stage. It was close to a full five minutes before Isaac could calm the audience down enough to begin his speech. He went up to the microphone, and said, "My friends, we have come a long way together. And none of this would have been possible without you." The audience was again uncontrollable in their cheering, feet stamping and clapping. Over the top of all this, Isaac continued, "And we will build a better, freer, and happier world for all!"

That was when the shot rang out and Isaac slumped over the podium. A man ran out of the room before the security guards could do anything and pandemonium erupted in the room.

You can only imagine the panic and anger that followed

immediately after these events. Within seconds Marko and Eric had ushered the VIPs out of the room, and all other leaders from the newly created nations were also rushed to safe rooms. The panicked crowd fled. In the days that followed, no one would be able to find out how the man got through security or how he evaded capture afterward. But the world lost its hero Isaac from his movie of life.

The movie of life is close to the end now.

"I want to become human. They need a leader. This is the moment we choose to help and not just watch."

Abdiel waited as she looked directly into the eyes of the ancient angel. It was not unprecedented to choose to become human, but it was unusual. It had been Marko's idea. He knew they needed a leader. He had originally asked Ithuriel, but Ithuriel had said no, preferring to focus on the people of the Western Union. And so Marko had turned to Abdiel. The angel had watched events unfold on earth and knew what was at stake.

"Yes Abdiel, I give you permission. Lead them with wisdom, courage and above all humanity."

Abdiel returned to earth, and made the permanent transformation to human form. At her request, Marko had arranged a meeting of the membership of the new global organisation and she made her request to take Isaac's place. Of course Ithuriel supported her, and many of the other leaders had respected Isaac for freeing them from their oppressive governments. They saw in Abdiel a light and a goodness that warmed their hearts, and they agreed. After the appropriate time, in a smaller, albeit well publicised event, Abdiel became the head of the new global organisation.

At the after party, Abdiel heard a familiar voice greet her, and turned to see Ithuriel.

"My friend, how good to see you. It seems you are not the only fallen angel around here."

Ithuriel replied, "I was feeling lonely, so I am very glad to see you my old friend. May we talk, privately?"

Nodding, Abdiel led Ithuriel into a side room. He began, "Abdiel, let me help you create a system that can truly last. Together, our vast knowledge will ensure a lasting peace. Let us take Isaac's dream and make it a reality."

Abdiel smiled as she remembered a different Ithuriel. Nonetheless, she was grateful for the support. "Yes,

Ithuriel. I believe that is a very good idea indeed." And so for the next 50 years the two great leaders created a society that would last well beyond their rule, a new international order based on rules, equality and trade.

Had divine intervention been necessary for these changes? I suspect not, but the best among us come from places of wonder, and I like to think they are angels come to help humanity. For this was not truly a story about Isaac and his ideals. It was a story about humanity and the potential we all have to change the world. Did Isaac have to die? I suspect not, and if you prefer, you may change this ending. A story's ending is chosen by the author, but it's the reader's imagination that is the ultimate critic. However, whether Isaac lived or died was not the point. This story was about the goodness that exists in humanity, and the belief and need to always strive for something better. It is about the individuals among us who rise to the challenge and meet their destiny with purpose. But more importantly, it is about all of us who individually fight for our freedom, who are the true hero and heroine in our own movie of life.

Epilogue.

The last word of this movie of life belongs to the author.

Our story was lived only once, but dreamed a thousand times, and our characters learned more than a million wondrous things. In an addictive way, we searched for answers we are not meant to find about the men, the monsters and the god who created the eternal world. For this world is our ideal place, one we seek to replicate in both our minds and lives. These worlds are the places of folklore, the places in which we create our very own Gardens of Eden, Fountains of Life and Trees of Destiny. These and many more such symbols and images all live within ourselves in a world that by its very definition and nature is a world beyond any possible conception or comprehension.

There is not one among us who can truly say they are wise. All we can seek to do is to be conscious of our actions and thoughts. While we may be jealous of those angels who live forever, we must remember that they live without the sense of touch, smell or true beauty, while humanity is able to find strength in its flaws.

Remember that in the end an angel had to become human to save us.

This was a story of humanity growing up, a story filled with emotion, raw and unbridled. Yet, it was also a story of understanding, of knowing that to be human is to be both flawed and ingenious. To recognise that it is both our actions in prayer as much as it is action in our laboratories that defines life. What this story means for our relationship with god, with each other, and with ourselves, is a question for you, the reader, to consider. If god did indeed create us, then this is us recreating god in our minds. This is humanity's way to reflect on life, and on death, for an eternity.

This work of literature was more than simply a story, more than simply entertainment. It was a work of philosophical fiction by your author. It was simply an exploration of the spectacle that is known as the movie of life.

ABOUT NATE HENDERSON

Nate Henderson is an Australian writer and diplomat. Nate has lived and worked in Australia, Asia, the Pacific, and the US. Nate has a wide ranging view of the world in which we live and aims through his work to both entertain and challenge readers to learn more about our amazing world.

Nate publishes under his own label, Jihona Publishing.

Connect with Nate

I would love to hear from you, so feel free to contact me with your thoughts and ideas at www.jihona.net.

This work is a Jihona project: changing the world through ideas.